The black stories

Amarabhilash

ISBN 978-93-5458-238-7
© Amarabhilash 2021
Published in India 2021 by Pencil

A brand of
One Point Six Technologies Pvt. Ltd.
123, Building J2, Shram Seva Premises,
Wadala Truck Terminal, Wadala (E)
Mumbai 400037, Maharashtra, INDIA
E connect@thepencilapp.com
W www.thepencilapp.com

Author biography

Amar Abhilash Samanta (born: December 26, 1996 (1996-12-26) [age 24]) is an Indian YouTuber who primarily uploads technology reviews.

Personal life

He was born on December 26, 1996 in Angul, Odisha, India. He is currently a student.
instagram :- Login • Instagram (Answering genuine queries on instagram.)
twitter :- Amar Abhilash Samanta (@iamarabhilash) (Answering genuine queries on Twitter)
cheak out other Twitch
Check out my youtube channel 👋😊
YouTube :- Amar Abhilash
Check out gaming videos 🎮
AmarAbhilash live

CONTENTS

Horror stories Part 1

So,at the start of the movie, we are shown a cave. A man is breaking it. Because he has murdered a lady. Now he wanted to hide her there. At night he buried her there and leaves from there. But after it, the voices of that lady come from the cave. The people get scared. And after that whoever passes by that cave that person disappear. This means that person didn't return from there. Now the scene changes towards a woman. Her name was kiara. And she was shifting to a town with her family. She comes here because her 5 years old son has died. And she became sad after this incident. The place where they shifted there was a deep forest in front of the house. There was an area and it was forbidden to go there. That area is surrounded by a boundary so that none can go inside it. Now let me tell you that this place was none other than that cave area. Kiara's mother-in-law also lives with them in the town. There was kiara's husband her daughter and her mother-in-law in her family.

Her mother-in-law was suffering from some kind of mental disorder. But kiara takes care of her very much. Kiara's mother-in-law has the power that she can listen to the voice of the dead ones. Due to it, she often talks strangely. After it, we see two kids a boy and a girl. Their cute puppy was lost. To search their puppy they were dividing posters. While searching for there puppy they reach that cave. There was dark in that cave. She turns on her mobile torch and sees inside that cave. She feels like someone is moving in the corner. With it, someone pulls that kid inside that cave. When kiara hears the noise she calls the police. And when the police go inside the cave they find a dead body of the girl there. There was a photograph near that dead body.

Kiara was also in the forest with her husband. She finds a baby girl there who was dirty and was also scared. The name of the baby girl was Amrita. Kiara went to her home with her husband and the baby girl. Give her bath. Then she notices that wound marks on her back .Kiara tries to talk to her but she wasn't saying anything. Suddenly the baby girl said kiara was her mother. For the first time the baby girl says something and kiara was shocked because baby girl voice is resembling kiara's daughter voice. Kiara's husband says to her that we should tell the police about the lost baby girl. Kiara says no I've lost my son already. What police had done? I have found amrita in place of my son. The days were passing by the bonding and attachments between kiara and amrita was becoming strong. Kiara loves amrita very much. One day kiara's husband asks her that how many days will we keep this baby girl in our house? We have to send her. Kiara says no I will not let her go. And if you want her to go I will also leave the house with her. She starts weeping. Her husband says to her that see we have to accept it. That our son is not in this world. And no-one can replace him.

control yourself I will support you. Kiara did not agree

with it. She says that I will take my son back for sure. One day kiara's mother-in-law has suffered from a psychological attack while sitting. She moves towards amrita with a knife. Then kiara arrives there and save the baby girl amrita. Here is the back story of kiara's son, one day kiara left his son alone in the hospital chamber but the bad luck is there's a acid chamber. Doctors use that to test it to give forensic report about any dead body and that day kiara's son was playing near the chamber and he tried to get a flux to play but the acid flux fall in the kiara's son and he died we know that about kiara and her mother-in-law conversation. Back to the present time, there's a mirror in the room of kiara's mother-in-law. They had totally covered that mirror. Because kiara's mother-in-law has the power that she can listen to the voice of the dead ones. And from the mirror she hears her dead siblings voice. Then horrible face is shown in that mirror. Like it is of a demon or soul. Kiara's mother-in-law starts talking to herself. And she started walking towards the forest hurriedly. She reaches that cave area where it was forbidden to go. It seems like someone is taking her there while pulling her.

the next morning, when kiara wakes up she sees that her mother-in-law is not anywhere. She tells her husband. When he goes to his mother's room and cheeks the mirror there was some fluid coming out of that mirror. Kiara's husband removes all the tapes from that mirror. There he sees the handprints of someone in that mirror. He thinks that from when this baby girl arrives at our house there is happening wrong. He goes to amrita and asks her that do you know where is grandma? After it , we see kiara's husband was also missing. Kiara gets confused and calls the police. She says that I don't want to live here. This is a strange town. She tells the police that I also have found a girl from the forest her name is amrita. Then police check in their record the missing report of this name girl. But they didn't find any missing report with this name. On the other side, kiara was taking amrita to meet with the police. But amrita was misplaced and she wasn't anywhere. The police tell kiara that for the past few days many people are missing. This town is mysterious. They also show that photograph to kiara. That they found near that dead body. Kiara recognize that this girl is amrita. When police check their old reports. They come to know that many people have seen this baby girl in the forest . When kiara was searching for amrita, she meets with a lady. That lady tells her about the cave.

A strong witch who is the most powerful one lives there and in a war of bad witches and good witches she lost her mortal body and a black magician gives her a tigress body where she lives forever young and nobody can defeat her. After it ,the white tigress want to protect magicians and give them more power and powerful enchantments. Then the magicians worshiped this white tigress. Among those magicians when a magician worship this tigress, the tigress wanted to take his soul and enter in his mortal body. But the magician had to save his life .So he started performing rituals on it. The magician throws his blood on a mirror but the tigress didn't like that blood. Because she wanted pure soul. Due to it, the magician sacrificed his daughter means amrita. After it, they were disappeared. After that day, the people were becoming disappear. The police officers find some photographs of amrita also. They come to know that magician beats amrita and physically abused her. That lady tells kiara if you have seen that girl then she will surely see the magician. Because they are the slave of tigress. You shouldn't take that girl to your house. That lady tells kiara that she can also posses you. And maybe you will loose your eyesight. Because this is it's first symptoms. And you will kill your own family members. Kiara's was already not seeing it properly.

The lady asks her to move from there. Kiara's daughter was alone at home so she immediately moves to her house. At home, her daughter was listening to her mother's voice means kiara's voice from the mirror side. That come here and don't scare. In fact, he was a magician who is in the mirror. He was calling kiara's daughter near him because she wants to hunt her. Kiara's daughter was scared and locks herself into a cupboard. Amrita says to her that don't scare I'm with you. She also sits with her in the cupboard. After reaching home, kiara starts searching for her daughter. But she couldn't find her anywhere. When she opens the cupboard she sees her daughter. She also sees amrita there. She thinks that amrita was taking care of her daughter. Kiara asks amrita that daughter can you tell me where are my husband and his mother? With it, she gets ready to move outside. And she leaves a card of police officer near her daughter. She says that if I will get late and couldn't come till morning so contact him . Amrita was taking kiara to that cave. In there conversation we had to know what actually happened with the magician and tigress. Actually tigress wanted to return so she demanded the magician soul and want to get control of his body. But the magician know the tigress went currpted and if the old most powerful witch come to the world there will definitely destruction of everything in everywhere.

So he performed a ritual to transfer the witch soul into another animal but the tigress get angry and make the magician and his daughter as slave and wanted destruction so she started killing people by their slaves. Back to the present time there was the old stairs in that cave. Those were horrible. Amrita asks kiara to go down slowly, quitly from these stairs. Amrita says to her that if you listen to any voice don't give any reaction. But then while walking kiara's foots get twisted. And she screams slightly. After her voice, the voices surround the whole cave. Her daughter and her husband were calling her towards them. Kiara hears her daughters voice from a corner. That mother comes here,here is horrible man. And I'm scared. Hearing her daughter painful voices kiara's heart melts. She says to her daughter I'm coming. And then she moves towards that place. But amrita stops her forcefully and asks her not to go there. Then that magician comes here who was possed by the tigress .He was about to kill them. But they hide in the part of that cave .While going to that place kiara's foots get stuck somewhere .that magician tries to come near her. But somehow kiara get her foot free. And runs from there. Then he takes out kiara's husband voice and says her to come to me. Now, amrita and kiara were in the room where there were a lot of mirrors. A hand comes from the mirror which was on the floor and it puts it on kiara's hand. To hold her.

but kiara run from there while getting released her hand

.There were voices coming from every mirrors. Kiara puts her hand on her ears because she was irritating. Because she was remembering her dead son. Kiara standing with a mirror . From which that magician tries to pull her inside . Means inside the mirror. And then the tigress will be in the world or having 3 slaves. But then kiara's husband arrives there and while saving kiara he breaks that mirror. Here we see kiara's husband become blind person. He says kiara to leave that place. Kiara was coming out of that cave. Meanwhile she received the call of that police officer .She was trying to tell him everything. But call disconnected. And she again falls down. Now kiara and kiara's husband try together to move out of the cave. But that magician who is changed now into a creature and he was having white hair on his face. He tries to drag her husband down. But kiara herself pulls her husband upside . Now kiara and kiara's husband were moving outside but they hear amrita voice from behind. She says mother you were saying that you will never leave me . Now, why are you leaving? Please don't leave. But kiara don't trust amrita right now . Here kiara also lost her light of eyes means kiara and her husband both are blind now. They both while holding each others hand try to move upside.

but those stairs were too much they were not ending. Then she hears the voice of her dead son .He says that mother doesn't go again leaving me. Hearing it, kiara heart started melting .But her husband says that you know that he is dead. And he is not here. Kiara again climbing up with her husband. But this time her son says sadly. Mother don't go. And here she lost her patients. She leaves her husband hand and says that I will soon bring my son back upside.

Sorry, going to downstairs kiara meets amrita. She hugs her. And then they moved inside the cave somewhere. On the other hand, we see kiara's husband who was successful to come out of the cave. But kiara is still missing. Now the cave was sealed .with it the book story comes to its end.

Now the second story, as the story starts we see a group of people who were the cult members. They bring their group leader to a lady's house. Because someone has possess their leader. And he was getting treatment from anywhere. They come here to this lady's house because this lady has many abilities. And she can make anyone free from the curse. So they force that lady to take out all evils from there leader. They gave her something to read. So that the other world door will open. And those evils will go there. Those were small spells. As that lady started reading them a dagger comes out of the mouth of that leader. That was deeped in the black blood. It means that the door of the other world is open. But then the police also get information about it. They come there and shoot them. Due to which the ritual remain incomplete. And because of that ritual that lady died. That lady who was reading the spells. And the police rescue her husband and daughter from there. Nothing is shown further. The scene changes to the other side. We see a student who was sleeping in her classroom. She was sleepy because she also does a part time job.

The circumstances of their house were not good. And she has to buy some medicines for her father. The name of the girl is Luna. One day, Luna was doing her work in the store. Meanwhile her male friend arrive here. He also studies in her school. He says to her that Luna the building in front of your store are you seeing? We all want to go there. As that building was abandoned so the security guard not letting us go inside. And you know him so please help us. Then one more girl arrive there. She was the friend of that boy. She requested Luna to come with them. In return, you can take my earrings. So Luna agrees. Then she goes with them to that building. They go to the sixth floor of that building. There were 2 more girls with Luna. Three boys are also with them. They were friends. It was the same place where that ritual was performing at the start of the story. And after that there was a great war and then this place was abandoned. This place was banned. Going there they started making videos. There are still signs those were made before the ritual . The page of that book were also there from which that lady was reading. Luna can also read those pages. She was no-one other than that lady's daughter. She was rescued. They all were standing on that symbol. That symbol was made for the ritual. Luna picks a paper from there to see that can she read or not? As she picks and reads it the symbol change into a portal.

That place is open. There was a lot of water. And they all fall in it. This means six students. After this happens on the other side Luna comes out of the water. She finds herself in a forest. She was scared. On the other side, we see the others were came out of that portal. But they see Luna and that girl who gave earrings to Luna weren't with them. On the other side there was dark in the forest. And many dark spirits attack Luna . Then Luna holds her mobile phone and its torch turn on as its light falls on that spirits it starts burning. And the spirit leaves Luna. Now the left students on the sixth floor go to the security guard. They say to him that our 2 friends were left upstairs. They were stuck in a portal. Then the security guard says that at first, you go into an abandoned building without my permission. The second thing is that stop joking with me. There is no place there like someone can be stuck in the portal. He doesn't help them. Now the other side of the portal, Luna was walking worriedly. Then she sees a huge building. It was a castle .She goes inside it and she sees that girl who gave her the earrings. Her name was Jessica. She was hanged in the air. There were strange woman near her. Luna immideatly goes and make Jessica free. Jessica gets scared and says how I come here? They were talking. Meanwhile ,that woman who hanged Jessica in the air comes near them. She starts beating them.

She was attacking them. Her ski was weird and her eyes were blank. This means they have turned white. Luna again hits the idea that why don't I check while throwing light on her? And she does the same . So the lady feels pain. That strange lady takes out the dagger . Like we are shown in the ritual. She was about to kill them. But Luna holds the dagger and kills that lady with it. Now Luna says to jessica that we have to go from here immediately. But before this ,the sister of that strange lady comes. The lady who attack them. She was also very strange. But they both run from there. Luna says to Jessica that we have to jump into the pool immideatly. So that we can return to our world. With it, Luna jumps in the pool. But when Jessica tries to jump she automatically drags towards that castle. Now the other side, In the real world, all friends of Jessica were worried.

They somehow take the security guard with them to the sixth floor. They say to him that see this was the pool in which we went. Our two friends are still inside it. The bodies of those girls coming on the book pages. This means they come to know that they are alive and inside it. But the security guard says that doesn't make me a fool. Maybe there is some leakage or you maybe you fill the water in this place after digging. How would I know that you come here for the first time or you often visit her? One of the boys says to a security guard that hasn't you study science?

And you know very well that it is sixth floor how can we dig it? That it makes a deep pool with deep water. They were talking meanwhile there a hustle bustle creates in that pool. Luna comes out of it, they all become happy that maybe they both will come out. They take her out of the pool. Then Jessica comes out and she was faint. But as she opens her eyes they were blank. Like that lady ,they were turned white. Because now she posses by the spirit. There was an axe in Jessica's hand . When that security guard comes in front of her she cut his hand with that axe. Luna turned on her mobile phone torch .She sees that there is a spirit behind Jessica. And that is controlling Jessica . It was clear from it that a spirit comes into this world with Jessica. Now that spirit starts screaming. That return my thing to me .They couldn't understand anything and now Jessica become aggressive. This means that spirit.she pushes the guard into that pool. She was making them all scared. They all run from there. But Luna was not going from there . Maybe she is feeling that she can make everything fine here. Getting a chance from it, Jessica moves towards her and starts attacking her. But one of the boys saved Luna and takes her with him. But Jessica holds that boy. And pushes him to the pool. Here Luna was scared .She tries to turn on the torch of her mobile again. But she couldn't do it . Jessica kicks her and throws her far. Then one more boy from Jessicas friend comes there.

But the directly falls in the pool. But before he goes to the other side of that portal he holds Jessica. Jessica also goes with him to the other side of the portal. Luna was there and she was faint. When she comes to her senses she sees that the there was no-one. She goes outside and turns on the torch of her mobile. When she comes out she sees that her friends were hanging in the air. They were saying Luna to help them. Save us Luna. Luna gets confused while seeing it. She couldn't understand that what to do. And then she opens her eyes and she was scared. This means it was a dream. There were two friends around her. Then they hold the pages of that book and start reading . Because they wanted to know that how can we take back our friends from that portal? Luna suddenly remembered that she has kept a dagger with her in her bag. When she saving Jessica. That lady who was attacking them. After snatching dagger from her and killed her with help of dagger . Then she kept the dagger in her bag. she immediately take out that dagger from her bag. So a boy standing there snatch that dagger from her.

He stars staring at it as he knows it. They think that creepy lady and that spirit who comes out with Jessica. The thing which she was demanding was that dagger. We have to return this dagger to her. Then she will spare us. But that boy who took that dagger from her, he says that no we will not give any dagger to her. And if we will still stop here she will also kill us. We have to leave from here. He is becoming man here. But now they don't have any choice or other options. Because there is no way to open the portal. They think that we should leave this building right now . And we will also save our friends. But the walls of the building were high. And all ways were closed. The keys is with the security guard fall to that portal so they're trapped. But suddenly Luna remember that Jessica has cut his hand. That key was in his hand.After taking the keys,she opens the door. But before they reach there, Jessica was standing with that axe, she was looking horrible. Now the surprise thing is that portal was closed and Jessica also went inside how can she come back? Maybe when Luna was faint and her friends were no there. The portal again opens.

Maybe Jessica comes again. Being scared they go to that room where was the portal is. They see portal was opened. This means not before Jessica comes right now. The dirty water was moving speedily in this portal. As it wants to drag everyone inside it. The Jessica holds a girl there. She starts cutting her neck with that dagger. That she snatched from Luna. But here Luna again turns on the flashlight of the phone .Due to it, Jessica starts burning. And she falls in the pool. That girl was also with her,whom neck was she about to cut. But that dagger falls down from Jessicas hand. Luna immideatly lifts that dagger again . Here Luna doesn't scare . She jumps in that portal with the dagger. Now she was swimming in the water. There was the castle on the other side, then she immediately come to that castle. She sees that her other friends who were fell in the portal were hanged in the air. And it is done by that spirit . Meanwhile, that weird horrible lady who was the sister of that lady comes by following them. She comes and ties Luna with a chair. She has sharp teeth. And her mouth was bleeding. She was near Luna as she will finish her. Luna again turns on the torch of her mobile again. As the lady takes a step back Luna runs from there while escaping her life. But that weird lady starts doing some magic. Due to it, Luna was falling. Luna was fell down and that strange lady was going near her. To kill her forever. But the male friend of Luna stabs her from the backside. He takes Luna and comes from there. Due to the pain that weird lady runs from there. They see the portal is closed now. That boy asks Luna to speak those spells to open the portal. Why you put us in trouble? Even you can do everything . how mean are you why did you put us in the trouble? But Luna says to him how mean are you?

Your other friends are hanging in the air we have to save their lives as well. Then we will go out from here. That boy says to Luna that I will kill you. Luna says that how can you kill me? Then that boy says that you don't know me that who am I? Do you remember when cult members brought their leader? And couldn't save them that leader was no-one other than my father. If your mother wanted she can save my father while saying those spells before. But she was doing dramas. I will take my father's death revenge . And you were thinking that why I need that dagger? Now you must understand that why I needed the dagger. I want to bring my father back to this world. It didn't happen then but now it will happen. But Luna pushes him. And says I will save my other friends. Even they were not Luna's friends before but now they have become friends. She release them all. She takes them with her. They come out of the castle. And start running towards that pool. On the way, the spirits try to stop them but they were running together . And saving each other life's. They see there was no pool and all the portals were closed. Then Luna starts reading those spells from that paper. Then the hustle bustle starts in the pool. The water starts appearing there. Now Luna says to everyone to jump in this pool one by one. A girl and a boy among jumps in the pool. But the boy who wants the dagger asks Luna that where is that dagger ? Luna says that may be it is left behind so that boy immideatly goes back to pick up the dagger. But then the horrible lady arrives there. She threws that boy at a far distance while using her power and energy. Then she also makes Luna falls. And sits on her. Her mouth was bleeding dirty blood . But during this Luna also got some power . Because she was the daughter of that mother who had many powers.while using power she pulls the dagger towards her. And stabs it in the neck of that horrible lady. Due to it, she starts disappearing. Then Luna starts running while taking Jessica with her but she didn't take the boy who wants the dagger tiwards to the pool. They jump in to it and then it is shown that they have come to their world without the boy. The portal was closed. Luna was a good girl she says that she will also take that boy back she starts reading the spells from that book. But now the portal wasn't changing. This means that boy will never come to this world. Now they all came out of there in their car.

Now the third story, there is a boy who is very good at all. Means that boy looks good, good scores in exam and goods at sports. He is very hard working boy. The boy named Anil. He gave a party on his birthday in abounded area. The boys friends were surprised and had many doubts why Anil gave his birthday party in abounded area? They confronts Anil with their questions but Anil answer that in that area his father has a beautiful farm house and no one have house in that area to stop doing party etc. So he gave his party in that area. He invited all his college friends. The party was held at his farm house . Everyone reached there at 6pm onwards . There was hustle and bustle. A big cake was placed on the table. All of them stood around the table and Anil cut the cake with the knife . All of the friends chanted three times ,"happy birthday Anil ". Then everyone set to eating. The cake was served to all. It was very testy. There were many things to eat. In the waiting room everyone sit there and started talking to each other but Anils friend has different mind. He announced that he wants to play game with everyone . So everyone was happy so Anils friend brought a CD player and a CD and says we all watch this then the game will start. His father was recently returned from his last traveling journey with the CD. His father told that it's the CD of devil and anyone who watches the CD he will crushed with 100 rulls and it only lifted by tomorrow morning .

He convinces all friends there that we will play it on a projector. Strange images begin to appear as she turns on the projector. As these are hypnosis images .That girl starts weeping ,glimpsing Those images. And everyone feels awkward. Then the boy who is the friend who plays the CD stands on the terrace of the house and jumps off. All friends are left shocked, seeing it . Now Anil call that boy who plays the CD with his name that is siru. And Anil started arguing with him but he calms down. Then a friend of Anil calls to rescue in confusion but he also faces something strange. He cuts his vein. And the bleeding is started from the wrist .At first sight , 5 friends commit suicide or unnatural thing. Then siru comes infront of everyone and says that everyone is going to die because they didn't help siru's girlfriend when some other friends in college started raging so it's everyone karma they didn't help his girlfriend now he or anyone else not helping them . After this some friends attack siru and try to kill him then the friends who went to kill siru they all died coz murder or attack someone is one of the signal so they died. Siru know all the signs of the CD so everyone tries to know that but siru confused . And went to his room.

Then everyone forces Anil to go to him and convince him to tell all 100 signs of the curse. But when Anil went to siru room,he saw siru is already died because after knowing all 100 signs he did one sign that is drinking water and he died. He wrote a letter and from that letter Anil know that everyone is forcing siru and no-one is helped his girlfriend so if he stays alive everyone will irritate him and confused him so in order to punish everyone he must die so he died. After it, everyone is going scared and worried about it. As a girl going to call her mother as being scared. But she killed. She pulls her tongue and died. Witnessing it, a girl started crying but she is also become the victim . Because crying is also a sign . Now all friends are thinking whether they may kill ,stepping out of the room. Then a boy named wada says to all that, don't be afraid! I check going out of the room . And when he goes outside , fortunately he gets no harm. Then he instructs all students that they will move outside. Because it's only a single way to get rid of from the teacher. All friends begin to move out of the room. And they had reached the school main gate. But a girl among them cross that main gate before .And that innocent ones is killed. All students begin to shout in fear.

But as abandoned area no-one come to help them. How they may protect him. So they began to plan themselves. They say ,we will have to investigate this at the very beginning . From where did the CD come? We may understand if we read about this in past history . Now they all start to gather the data about him from computer as well as from library and siru room where he last found . But no-one gets information except Anil and wada. They had found out a book from siru's bag. There was information about those images in that book. With the collection of them ,a video was made. And they watch it on the projector. This video was released by a cult. The people are get hypnotized ,watching it. So we have been hypnotized after watching it. It has 100 signals as was told by siru's father. Luckily ,50 signals have been already been written in this book.it means that we will have to easy to what to do and what not to do. They write these 50 signals along with the experience signals on the board. They also decided that they will also know the other signals. So 4 friends go in search of another book. Some of the students go there, taking something to drink . But they also commit unnatural thing. Because there was also a signal. There were forbidden to drink. And wada and Anil didn't reveal that signal to them.

In fact there were 60 signals in that book. And wada informed them 50 signals. Because he wants to kill the other students ,using the other 10 signals .And he wants to be a survivor at the end. In the same way, he kills a girl. Then Anil comes to wada. He says I have witnessed everything. You are becoming very smart! I have also got a book. And I have known all other 60 signals. When other students known that the girl with wada had met her end, then they suspect wada may know the other signals. And he is not revealing us! So he remains the survivor. All students began to ask questions from wada. But he asks why are you suspecting over me? I'm also a friend like all of you. Why will I do wrost with my companions? Then his companions says to him, no one care for others lives if he Only has to Survive in the end, but he is not agreeing their opinion. Two of students among them suspect him confirmly. They offer him to drink, going after him. They declare ,We have listened that it is also one of the signal to not drink. That you didn't reveal to us! Just drink it to confirm. So wada says, okay! I have no issue to drink! You may also drink as I take. Nothing will happen. And wada drinks before them. So he gets no harm. After that boy also drink who had come after wada. But he began to feel something along with it. And he commits unnatural things while stabbing the bottle in his tummy.a girl named kriti is witnessing everything. she observed that wada had not drunk. he had not let water inside his body. kriti tells them when 2more friends arrive there.

That wada is very wicked boy. he was the same who killed that girl. on the other side ,Anil who had found the next book. he tells other students wada deceiving us! there were total 60signals we read together. but a boy snatched the book from her hand. And starts reading while opening it. but it is a cartoon book. that boy thrust an electric bulb in to his mouth. he gets electric shock and he died. it is also a signal that you can't read cartoon books and graphic novels. Anil tell them, that it was a part of my plan. I have still the original book and I also know other signals. then wada approches there. But Anil says wada is lying there was 100 signals and argue with wada why he was lying to everyone. he says all of them, you will have to join my group if you want to survive and if you wants to know other signals. And I will not victimized him who will be in my group at first. it means that they are little secure. some of the friends are getting angry on wada. but they don't want to be angry otherwise they also be get killed. so then they divided in groups. some of friends comes in group of wada. Now wada tells them a strategy of which was among those signals. that person will be ended if all seven point a finger to a person. Now wada and his six group members point there fingers to a friend. And that poor one strangles himself.

Now kriti begins to leave from there ,taking her friend. so that they may search for others signals. they witnessed of two friends on the way. who had helds the hands of each other. and they are looking into the eyes of each other .but they are not alive. it means that their friend used to forbid them to look each other in the collage. it was also one of the signal in those signals. that you may be killed if you keep looking into the eyes of anyone for a longer time. kriti and her friend moves in to the room. where the game was started. they gradually began to learn all the signals . which was instructed by his friend in college. in this way, it takes the form of 100 signals. kriti tells his friend, we go to wada. there was a envious girl in the group of wada. And they all together started to point there finger to kriti. at the same time, kriti's friend also arrives. And they pointed there fingers on them. then wada is scared that I may not be killed. Anil also arrives with his group and pointed there fingers to wada's group. then wada stops all the companion. kriti tells her companion that , there was such signals which was not been reveal by the book. it is that you only have time till tonight.

We will all die as the down breaks. others will also not remains alive if one of us not survive among us. Now the companion of wada feel aggressive towards him. that he hide that fact from them. they come to attack him. but wada hits upon a plan. he sheilds himself ,wearing the rain coat. And he started to throw the alcoholic drinks on the other friends. as a result ,all students begin to die along with Anil. now that envious girl is also moving towards kriti. so he may kill her. but alcoholic drinks also spilled over her and she commit suicide or unnatural things. now there are only four friends or survivor in the house . all other friends had been killed . Now kriti, wada and two male friends were survived. the friend who was with kriti in her room, wada takes along with him. wada has a bottle filled with blood . he says to that boy, we will have to sacrifice here. I'm repeating of my guilt! kriti is female and we will have to save her. so we both sacrifice ourselves, drinking this blood. because drinking blood was also one of the violence of these 100 signals. now wada clarify hands the bottle filled with blood to another boy. the guiltless boy is nearly to drink the blood. then one more boy comes to them which was one more survivors except three of them. he hits the bottle as he witnessed wada of doing so. as it has been told that they could only commit unnatural thing. it was violation of the signals to hurt someone or to kill. so that the boy of optical glasses become the victim .he commits unnatural things. seeing it wada stands and moves outside .now kriti and her friend move in to the laboratory. kriti's friend informs her, siru has some some tablets .these are same tablet to what extent I have investigated. that can remove this hypnosis ,but the problem is that these are only two. and we are three in number .why do we think ill for others? we should also tell about it to wada. so we mutually decided who is in the dier need of these tablets. now wada is on the top floor. and there was also going to down soon.

It means that time had left short. Now they both move to the roof. And they meet wada. kriti's friend reveal the whole fact to wada. without uttering a word, wada takes that tablet while snatching from him. kriti's friend says to him, you have fooled. it was an ordinary tablet. then the boy attempt to push wada from the roof. but wada also defend himself . the fight started between them during this time. which was wholly violation of the signals. And they both commit thing. wada jumps off the roof. while other boy wounds his eye, stabbing a scissor into it. and he is also no more because of the massive bleeding. kriti understand well . why did her friend do it? because he yarned to rescue kriti. now all friends come to an end . kriti was only survivor girl , who had survived among all of them . and hypnosis is removed from her. and her life remain secure. now it was also dawned. police arrived there when the friends don't reach their house after a day. kriti begans to report the whole incident. she tells siru is responsible for this ! but police doesn't get the dead body of the teacher while investigating. the police included that these all friends have committed suicide. and it also appearing the same. because everyone found evidence was indicating this. these are the suicidal deaths. so this case is not detected for a long time . and this case was closed because of weak evidences. in the end, it is seen that siru was sitting in a dark place .these cases of hypnotism were forgotten by the world and police . but kriti had everything in her mind. she used to miss her friends. so she always wants to take revenge. today she had found siru. she had the same projector and the compact disk. kriti turned on the projector . the same hypnotism images began to appear in front of her friend siru. and he also under the effects of hypnotism. he will soon commit suicide .

the fourth story, the story main character was 15 year old girl named Veronica. she used to live in Madrid with her mother and siblings in the year of 1991. his father was dead before a time. her mother used to work day and night in a club to run her house . Veronica had to take care of her siblings due to these circumstances. in the morning of June 12/1991,veronica is getting ready with her siblings for the school. and it was the day of solar eclipse. and students had to view the solar eclipse under the teachers guardianship. before the solar eclipse time, teacher's are telling their students in class about it. as what is solar eclipse . informing them ,teacher's also tell them that in ancient time, people used to sacrifice someone at the moment of /time of solar eclipse. moreover ,it was believed that the old persons spirit can be called in this world by anyone . while disscusing,it is also shown us in the class that Veronica was not interested to view the solar eclipse . rather she is planning something with friend Rosa. at one side, all students are moving upstairs to view the solar eclipse. while Veronica goes in the basement in the school with her friends Rosa and Diana. where they were conduct a seance. they want to contact with the spirit of anyone through spirit board. Diana yearned to call her friends spirit who was dead before a month in an accident. and Veronica wants to call her father spirit. first of all, they place Veronicas father photo in front of spirit board. and they attempted to contact with his spirit. three girls place the hand on a glass cup and also get the immediate response .

that glass cup began to move on the response of spirits. and that glass cup is too hot that Rosa and Diana pull their fingers back. Veronica was only who was accomplished this seance. that glass cup is broken at the time of the solar eclipse. Veronicas finger is injured and bleeds because of the broken glass cups . this blood is dripped on the spirit board. Veronica is silent like a dummy and that spirit board is divided into two parts breaking. meanwhile, the unusual activity are started in the basement. and Diana starts screaming. Veronica wishers of words lying down on the ground. and suddenly she shouts in satanic voice lossing her senses. then we are shown that Veronica is in the ward of her schools hospital. she is being checked by a doctor. doctor thinks that the reason of her unconscious is the iron deficiency. and she should be careful on her food. and when she is returning to house with her siblings , then she observes resident nun who is continuously starring at Veronica. people used to call this number death. and above all ,this nun was blind . now the question is aroused that how was she starring at Veronica .different things are happening with Veronica even reaching at house. she is frozen at dinner time. moreover the claws mark started to appear on her body. while bathing her brother Antonio, then she hears some sounds from her room. and she looked in that room pursuing these sounds. and she hears her brother Antonio's voice in that locked room.

anyhow, coming from the room, she moves into lavatory where Antonio is shouting in the bathtub. someone had opened the hot pipe valves as a result Antonio body was burned. then Veronica immideatly brings Antonio out the bathtub and uses ointment for burnt body. at the night ,Veronica dreams of her father who is calling her. then Veronica is pulled by the many apeard hands. Veronica father was also turned into a black ghost. and he orders to attack on her. after it ,Veronica is awakened. she finds everything normal. Veronica goes to school in coming day but her friend Rosa is ignoring her. after being upset ,she moves to basement and meets nun death. nun deaths inform her that Veronica has committed blunder calling the ghost spirit. while doing it, her fathers spirit didn't come in this world but Satan spirit. and that Satan is always with Veronica even still now. it is also reveal by nun death. that when she used to see satanic things before her. but she damaged her eyes after facing irritation. but she knew later that human sight is not necessary to view such things. before going, nun asks Veronica that you yourself have to take care and protect your siblings. Veronica draws protection symbols in all rooms after these occurances in orderd to keep satanic spirit far. but it doesn't happen as much ,that Satan burns all protective symbol easily. and her mother has saviour accident and her siblings were acting like possesed.

after this , Veronica and her friends do it again the ritual but they all suffer from pain during the ritual. Veronica is already possessed by the Satan so she can't control it but other two girls has halusinatic by the Satan. but they used a cup with gum so there hand must stay in the ghost board. the ghost board is split due to it, they see different things like Diana sees her parents are dead, her siblings scolded her. Veronica acting differently because she was possessed by the Satan so she could not handle the halusination her father transform into a demon and tourcher her brother Antonio. Rosa was silent and faint he could not handle so she cut her finger and ran away due to it another demon come to this world now Diana cut her finger and ran away from there, again the ritual remain incomplete. due to it there are two different demons come to life . they hunt Veronica and their siblings. one day Antonio was possessed by the second demon and try to kill Veronica. Veronica goes to nun death and seek help . nun death discovered that the demon is very week .it means that the second demon was very week. so she tries her way and the week demon goes away from where it comes. but then the Satan demon was very angry and try to fully possessed

Veronica body. the demon overpower Veronica and control her body but Veronica want to get rid of the demon. so she started to doing the ritual again with her siblings. but at first she goes to her friends and asks if they would help but they both were denied. Veronica is left alone . then she decided to conduct this seance with her siblings to get rid all these occurances . one day, that spirit is choking Veronica's sister throat to kill her. and Veronica attempts to save her. as a result, Veronica's sister was afraid and said that Veronica is choking her throat not anyone else.

Veronice explain on it that Satan has actually arrived in our house and it was doing this. and she just protecting her sister from it. Veronica again dreams at the same night. she dreams that her sister is eating her biting with teeth and her brother Antonio is also chocking her. and her mother is scolding her with it. and frightened all these Veronica is awakened. rising from her bed, she finds blood soaked bed .and there was black mark under the mattress . it was seeming, as that mattress has been brunt. while checking all mattress of the house ,she finds the same burn mark on all . and it was appearing from that mark as someone has tried to burn it. and above all,that black mark indicating a satan. Antonio tells Veronica that his father came to meet him at that night. and he said , I will bring you with me!! hearing it ,Veronica is afraid and relates to his brother , there is no need to follow anyone. and closing eyes and ears, he should call Veronica so that she may come . meanwhile, Veronica again meets nun death and asks help to get rid of this demon. and Veronica conducts Seance with her siblings after fixing the spirit board . and Veronica asks Antonio to draw protection symbol on the wall but he draws invocation symbol mistakly .conducting the seance, Veronica asks Satan to leave this world. but that spirit refuses . she tries to get the Satan out from this world reading different books. but he appears in complete figure before them attacking. Veronica call police in fear while Antonio is taken by Satan. veronica's sister lucia and Irene ran out of the house avoiding all these. while Veronica return back to her house in search of Antonio. then she knew that he is locked in her room .and she try to communicate with him. but Antonio does the same which was said by Veronica. closing his eyes and ears, he is calling Veronica . afterwards , Veronica feels awkwardness in herself.but reality was this, Satan is neither in this house nor in the house but in Veronica.

And this time, Veronica realises that a great secret is exposed here that antonio was brunt in bath tub by veronica. but she rescued her after coming to her consiousnesss.moreover,she was the same who was chockingher sisters throat. coming into senses,she stops all that. otherwise,veronica was the cause off all occurance at home. and the purpose of spirit was to posses veronica. when veronica come to know that she is the root of all happenings, then she tries to cut her throat with the broken piece of glass. but she is stopped by satan. police officers also arrives there duringt this situation. and pollice officers are left astonished seeing this occurance. because veronica's body was in the air. then she falls down lossing her senses.police officers brings antonio and veronica outside of the house. and they take veronica in ambulance.detectives look at the fallen things in surroundings. then suddenly they notice veronicas photo in a frame which is brunt immediately. then they get death news of veronica. she is no more. after that, the detective makes a report taking this case. here, he declares that the root of all these occurances was the spirit.who had come in our world because of incomplete seance. more surprising thing is that, it was the first pollice case where the spirit was mentioned.

the fivth story , a view of an english village is very greatfull to see.and three young girls were playing there. suddenly they catch a sight of something in the corner of that room. leaving their game and toys, they commit suicide jumping from the window. then the glimps of shadow in the room is viewed. then 8 years later of this incident, a boy named aurther kims is shown. at that time, aurther wife conceiving a child. unfortunately, mother is died after conceiving a child and the child is safe and sound. then kims has to move at a place in case of selling his eel marsh house after 4 years of this incident. and giving responsibility of his son to his caretaker, he moves towards that place. then it is revealed through conversation that kims son and care take has a plan to visit at kims house to meet him after 4 days. kims meets a wealthy business man on the way. he used to live at the location where kims was going. when kims expose the propose of his arrival, that businessman tells that he will not get the buyer of eel marsh house. it means that house cannot be sold. kims astonished to hear it but he ignored. at last he reaches his hotel. reaching there, kims asks from the allotted room there from the receptionist. he refuses to alot the room but receptionist's wife agrees. the same room is alloted to kims where three girls had commit suicide after jumping. next morning, kims meets a person who was tackling all the dealings and the documents off eel marsh house. that person doesnot please to meet kims. he says,it is in vain to come here because he was dispatching all document there.he hands him the documents while taking. he tells kims that he can catch the train soon for his return. he should immidiately leave from her. but he says to kim sending him outside that his car driver will drop him at the without hearing anything from kims. other villagers also dislikes the arrival of kims like the person , as they never wanted him to come and discuss about the selling of eel marsh house.

but kims had also internded to return after the completion of his task. offering money to catchman, kims asks to lead him towards the eel marsh house. eel marsh house is situated far away at a place. its surrounding was unpopulated having not a single house. there was only a graveyard near it. when kims inside the house, a black shadow is seen at his back side. turning back, kims find no one. ignoring it, he gets busy in his work while discovering the house. he looks at a lady wearing a black dress in the graveyard through a window. kims come downstairs for seeing that lady but there is no one. that coachman again comes to take kims at the evening time. returning back to village, kims reveals everything to a village constable who does not take it seriosly and he ignores. meanwhile, 2 little boys comes there catching a girl of their age fellow. they tells kims, she has taken something wrong so she is unwell! that little girl condition was worst. kims calls village constable loudly observing the condition of that little girl.

the village constable does not come for help and that little girl is dead. at the same night, kims visited that wealthy business man named mr.daily whom he met on the train. kims comes to know that Mr daily also had a son who passed away in his young age. Mr.daily tells kims something about his wife that sometimes she suffers the fits of hysteria acting mysteriously. he also reveals a strange fact as he says in the hysterical condition of his wife, she says that her dead son is trying to contact her through a mysterious power. but Mr.daily takes it pointless. he does not care for it and thinks as his wife is mentaly sick and talks and act like this, at the same night, Mr.daily"s wifeagain suffers the fits of hysteria and she carves something on table using a knife. seeing it, Mr.daily knocks her down giving the smell of chloroform to her. kims is shocked observing that photo because that photo was was giving a view of female suicider. kims goes to the dealer of eel marsh house in the coming day.but he is not at his house.

kims glimpses a locked little girl in the basementof the house.but that girl says, leave me alone! and go from here! swwing it, he come outside. many people block their way standing there when Mr.daily begins to take kims to eel marsh house. little girls father blames kims for her death who was died in the hands of kims. he was blaming kims because he had been seen that lady in eel marsh house. and that lady killed little girl. the rest of the villagers asks kims to return back to london but he was not leaving this place. Mr.daily takes kims at eel marsh house crossing his car among the villagers in any way. kims says to daily, he may spend the hole night here because of his work. hearing it, daily leaves his dog for kims. night falls until they reach the house and kandles the candles. kindling all the candles, kims starts reading the placed papers, documents and cards in that house. kims finds a letter in those papers which was for a lady named alice arthur who was the owner of this house. and the sender of her letter was not other than but her sister jannet. alice was childless. caling her sister mentaly sick, she had snatched her sister's child from her. it was also written in the letter that alice never allowed her sister to meet her child. jannet said, alice has snatched her child but the blood relation will remain forever. kims also finds there other letter which was from jannet to alice. the cauase of childs death was mantioned in that letter. jannet clearly blames her sister alice saying,she is a killer of her child. itwas written in the letter as she could save the life of her child if she wanted it. but she prefers her life than her child. kims also get death certificate of that child. and a great secret was reveald that it was the place of nursery where jannet commit suicide hanging herself. everything is crystal clear here. daily's dog was barking looking at the exit door. going outside, he notices that atmospheric condition is not normal. it is raining cats and dogs. and kims sees the dead children's souls in the direction of forest who were killed in the village.

observing it, kims returns to the house getting worried. kims checks a door at the top floor of house which does not unlock in spite of his efforts. then kims takes an axe for breaking that door. but he finds the automatically unlocked door returning back. he observes the rocking chair going inside. as it was moving as someone is sitting on chair. the chair is empty but moving. a lady suicider is viewed by kims when he looks up in the worried condition. she disappeared immidiately. kims frightened seing it. and a child ghost increases his terror. while escaping he encounters a black dressed lady coming towards him. escaping from her , he locks himself in a room. he notices as the black colour is dominating on the bed and a child ghost is emerging from there. he is scared coming outside the room. he moves downstairs frighteningly. he goes to main door to go outsidethen he finds Mr.daily standing there. actually, he was here to take kims. kims was confused in this disturbed situation that how did it dawn while discovering the house. he shares all happend events in the house with daily. but daily was nor ready to acceptr it as a truth. he was not trusting him. as the return back to village, they find the brunt house of eel marsh house dealer. kims faces a mysterious thing when he runs to basement in order to save the life of that mans girl. jannets soul was provoking that little girl for suicide. kims stops him but that little girl burns herself ignoring him. kims is left astonished seeing it and comes outside. he again moves to daily's house with him. where he began to meets daily's wife and knows that the cause of behind daily's son was drowing. meanwhile, daily's wife suffers the fits of hysteria. her voice is changed and she says, she makes to do it. then all children's death is shown who commited suicide when jannets soul provoked them to do it. at this time, daily also arrives there and his wife losses her senses in his hand.everything is cleared before kims as the black dressed lady is the wondering soul of jannet. and the porpose behind all this is to take revenge of the death of her child. kims thinks, why not! we should arrenge a meeting between jannet and her childs dead body! she will stop victimizing the child after getting the relief. daily refused his idea saying, it is not easy task!

Because her childs dead body has never been found. kims plan to search the dead body of that child in that marsh where he died. thinking it, he takes the way to eel marsh house. he ties the one side ofrope with him while other side with a car. he himself steps in that marsh. he gets the deadbody of that child after getting a great search. taking the dead body of that child, he places it in that room where he first time had the sight of jannets soul. kims had sorrounded that dead body with those letters and cards which were written by her. daily's faces his son's soul on the ground floor. pursuing him, he enters a room door magically loocked after his entrance there. daily's frighened and calls kims in fear. on the other side, kims was getting worried that jannet did not come here. to meet her loving son. then he feels the presence of someone. he observes tht all candle lights themselves are blowing out. he immidiately understands as jannet arrives. then jannet's soul really appears and swiftly moves to kims he falls down in fear. loocking at her child, she calmed down. he instantly returns back. and daily comes to kims as his door is unlocked. kims inform daily that jannet has left now. so our task is to bury the childsdead body with his mothers dead body. so this cruelty may stop here. she may got her child and her fire of revenge may extinguish here. they both move to train station after burrying the both dead boddies together. kims meets there with his son and caretaker. kims introduce his son with daily and asks caretaker to bring the tickets to london. kims says, they will not stay here even for a single day and leave for london in next train. kims was conversing wiith daily while caretaker was engaged in buying tickets. so kims attention is diverted from his son. that kid begins to move before the front coming train leaving the hand of his father. kims again sees the black dressed lady at a side. noticing his kid, he moves forwards to save life of his son. but father and son are crushed by the train at the meantime. then daily looks at the souls of all kids who were dead in the village including the soul of jannet. on the other side, kims again shown. waking up,he meets his decreased wife. and he leaves after taking her. both are pleased with each other. actually, kims and his son both were dead. there death of three unite their family and they are both happy together. after their departure, jannets soul again appears but she was looking sad now. it was seeming as she is regretfull on her doings.

the sixth story, her we see some vampires hunters. a prist was shown. in the same way, he is going in search of vempires at night. but vempires has set a trap for him and a prist is intrapped. it is tried to get him free but in vein. and he dies. then flash back comes, it is revealed a story. vempires and humans being used to live together. they used to protect each other. but they had a great contempt amoung them. they used to disdain one onother and continue their fighting everytime. the tranquility had discoverd in the city where these battles are going on. vempireshad started to kill the human beings. and this place was not without any risks for the human beings. because there was a great differencebetween the way of living of vampires and human beings. so humans being took a decision to secure their lives and their family lives too. they loocked themselves in a church so they may survive there securely. so they build the giant walls for this cause there so on one may approach there. so vempires may not cross these limits. there was a reputed prist. he was vigorous. he was honoured by all the prists. because the prist had the ability of everything. he could fight with vempires perfectly. when that prist knew that vempires created turbulance.so they locked vempires, capturing them. after this, tranquility prevailed throughout the city. no one used to fight. nor was there any vampires. so the people were free of fear of their life and family life due to this. but many clergies lost their profession for this cause. some of the clergies turned in to lower class, some started the field work. and they adopted the diffrent profession. somehow, they may earn thir living. now a family comes on the city including a couple and its daughter named lucy. that family was industrious. and it seemed as if they always re,ained in grief. One day that couple is dinning. then their daughter lucy comes from outside. her father shows his anger too much saying, lucy! where had you gone? lucy tells, father! i am comming from the city. lucy's father says to her, how many times i have forbidden you to not to visit city. you are insecure there. now lucy's mother calms lucy's father down. and she tells the etiquette of taking meal. they are communicating. that earth begins to shake similar like the earthquake. all they are frightened.

they all had come to know that, that vempires are about to approach. lucy's parents locks her in the cellar. while they themselves remains outside of the cellar. now there is an assult of vempires there. lucy's parents died. lucy begins to cry alot. and they take her with them after abduction. now turns and the priest is shown speaking. that he is sorrowfull. because one of their companions had victimized by the vampires. and they had not got courage to save her. then they encounter lucy's friend outside. who is an officer. and she used to save her by visit there to meet him. it means, this friend of lucy's used to live in the city. he starts to reveal the whole story to priest. that lucy is my dearest friend. but she has been taken away by the vempires. and the priest lucy's friend is taking about, that priest is the parental uncle of lucy . he tells,that lucy's mother was ended under the assault of the vampires. but her father or my brother is still alive. then lucy's friend says, i have to rescue my friend! i have listened about you! kindly help me! i have a dire need of your assistance. priest keep silent. he reveals the whole heard story to his masters, are directly moving to the church. that masters says, the vampires attack is incredible. they are all imprisoned. you know it well. how will they attack someone? priest cannot utter a word. he couldnot speak a single word. before his master. but it was clicking his mind, then who did abduct lucy? if vampires have not kidnapped. now the place is show where lucy is present. and it was truth that kidnapper of lucy was not anyone else but a human. he was savage. he warns lucy, you will not step outside from here. i will end you if you took this action. further, priest is show who is taking with his partner. that i have to go to rescue my daughter lucy! who is daughter of his brother. his partner says to him, you have also been forbidden by the master! you path will be full of threats if you violate him! it means that your task will be difficult. you will never be able to search for lucy. but the priest says, i will surely have to leave! who will rescue her if i don't do as such. they are still conversing, that two persons begin to attack them while arriving there. but the priest kills both of those persons very ingeniously. because he had no fear of anyone. he knews the techniques to fight with vampiers so humans were nothing before him. standing up, he promises that he will return after rescuing lucy.

he has the advance technological weapons and motorbike. he rides on that bike, taking all his weapons. he was very passionate to rescue lucy so he moves to her house. from where she had been abducted. afterwards, he alsdo takes lucy's friend with him. now they moves together to lucy's father who was badly wounded. here the priest gives his words to lucy's father that, i will come back after searching your daughter. priest says to lucy's friend befor departing it,it will be better me to go alone! but lucy's friend says, i am also skilled. i can also finish vampires. the priest says to him, which skill do you prossess? then he shows him the art of using the dagger. being inspired, priest also takes him along with him. when masters of church comes to know about it, then he feels very ill. he says that i will have to build a team to search for the priest. and he groups the other prists to build a team who is going to bring that priest after searching. on the other side, lucy and his friends are seen.they observes the footprints of someone on the way. the priest says, these are not appearing vampires footprints. it seems that these belong to any human being. they glimps of a man there who is badly cutting the chiken into pieces. he was preparing vampires food. then priest asks him, going there. whose footprints are these! is there any vampire here who has passed from here? then that man talks with them strictly. go away! i don't know. then the priest moves to a cellar, going inside.

there is fightfull man who begins to fear, seeing the priest. he asks, why have you come here? go away! hearing him, all present workers of that place also come there. and they had been imprisoned there for the security of that place. so they all people had come to attack priest and lucy's friend. but priest and lucy's friend also begin to attack them in return. and they began to kill them one by one. priest asks the last survived worker that, if you tell me about lucy,i will not harm you! that worker says, i don't know where is lucy. and he tries to tangel priest. so that night falls soon and vampires may appear. it happens the same. the night falls and many vampires begin to appear there. they had one sort of blade. lucy friend and priest begin to hit the vampires with it. at last, the time arrives, all vampires escape from there in fear. priest goes to the last survived worker and asks, will you tell me where is lucy? he informs that they had taken lucy to the west. meanwhile, a huge and horrible vampire kills that worker, coming there. so he may not tell whole adress of lucy. priest and the lucy's friend and his partner get agressive on it.but priest sits there with lucy's friend and plans how the acess may be got to lucy.

they began to find out the address on map and say, the way is very dangerous which leads to it. thy come to know where lucy has been taken, that place is very weird. it has a history. there was broken out a war and six vampires had survived. they were not killed because they were feeble. now they both reach that place. and they meet a man there who was devlish. they also ask him about lucy. then that man moves to a man who was a former priest. now he had turned into evil vampire. his name was black hat. he tells him that priest and lucy's friend are searching for you, because you have abducted lucy. blackhat flies into rage. he says, why are you telling me? why did you not takle yourself? he bites him so he is also transformed into vampires. contrarily, priest and lucy's friend are in the road. they move to a cave and hear the sound of something. there is a girl when they check it. she reveals them, master has grouped a team of priests to capture both of you, i was also among them! but i parted from them. but you need not to worry. i know that you are doing good. and lucy should be searched out. and i will help you in this matter. this is cause i told you that master wants to capture you. so that you may care it. that girl is a priestess. a huge vempires attacks them as they are moving ahead. but they defeat it after fighting. as they are moving forward, then priestess began to tell her story. as it has already been told when the war broke out among vampires,then the jobs of all priests were ended. they had turned into lower class. then this pristess had also started to swap the garbage. it means, her condition was also worst. now a priest who is along with priestess,he also tells, yeah! it happened the similar with all priests. and master did it bad. and he is still wanting to catch me because, i am searching for lucy. then they come to know coming out of the cave,that ther is an army of vampires ahead. and they can also attack them. but all the vampires went to a city before their coming out of the cave. and they started to kill all the people. there was also three priests there to stop them. but those vampires were vigorous, that they also kill three priests. and they fix their dead bodies on the crucifix. in the morning, when priest,priestress and lucy's friend reach here, they are grieved,witnessing the dead bodies of the other priests. they get understanding that vempires will soon attack us. now they all investigate how did these vampires reach there.

they come to know as they come here by train. now they begins make the weapons. so they will stop from coming here at any cost. on the other side, lucy and black hat are sitting in front of eachother. it asks her, will you take food? then black hat says to her, i tell you a story! you know! it was thought in the world that soul does not exists in vempires. only the human being is superb! but it was wrong. soul also exist in vampires which was more powerfull. clergymen shouldn't have killed vampires as such. now human beings feel trouble when vampires want to take revenge. now that time has approched that i may reveal to the world, that we have more need vampires. do yo know why i brought you here? so you may help in me in the whole task. i also know it that priest will surely come here to rescue you. and i will also take his help. on the other side lucy's friend is so sad, because he knew if lucy transformed into vampire before their acess, then priest will kill her. but the pristress consoles him, and she says, we need to live fort to the world! if you will lose ur courage thinking it, how will we carry out our oporation? now they start to move in that direction from where vampires were about to come. or there was treat of the approaching of the vampires. now they reach the railroad. then lucy's friend target priest with his gun and he says, no matter what happens! either my friend had transformed in to vampire, but you will not kill her. then priest says to him, okay! don't think as such. if i reveal the truth that I am the father of lucy. i told a lie to you that i am her uncle.

who can think better than me about my daughter. knowing it lucy's friend feels little relaxation. they are with the train and they have known that vampires are in it. they began to hide bomb there. that priest comes on the train roof. there is also black hat vampire. here the reality of black hat vampire is exposed. remember it was told at the first of the story, that a priest was entraped by vampires. and no one had got courage to rescue him. all thought that he was no more. latter, vampires themselves had saved him. afterwards, they turn him into the vampire like them. and they use it for themselves. when human and vempires soul mingled, so it became stronger. and that black hat turned into vampire.

then the great war started between priest and black hat. black hat kicks priest so he is fallen away. it means black hat is strongest. then many workers apear there. they were under services of vampires. they started to attack pristess and lucy's friend. but pristess defeat them. in the same way, black hat throws priest in to the train. there is lucy who was in the possesion of a vampire. she is screaming. priest tries to rescue her. lucy also burns him who had cought her. afterwards, black hat comes before her. lucy attempts to attack him using a knife. but black hat was very shrewd. he saves himself from the attack of knife. black hat injures priest badly, attacking with that knife. and it leaves, taking lucy. black hat had taken lucy on the train roof. where he was going to transform her into a vampire after biting her. but priest reaches the train roof, getting courage. he has a blade of crucifix which he threws directly on black hat. so lucy is going to fall from the train, lossing her balance. but priest rescues her. but black hat still wanting to finish priest. then pristess is rides bike and driving it spiddily. this sight is nice. she was driving bike before the train so there may be a good explosion with there collision. and it occures the same. as the fast driving bike collides the train, so the train explodes and all the vampires are died in it. fortunately, blackhat is no more. he had also been died. now the time after few miniute, when priest take lucy in his lap. lucy's friend also feels satisfaction after seeing lucy with no harm. and priest smiles while looking priestess saying, you did a great job. at last they had succeeded and they had also acomplished mission. and they had secured lucy. black hat was also not alive. in the end the priest who moves to the same master in the church. he trews a vampire head before him saying, I am returning after fighting with vampires. they want to harm us! you are still claiming, vampires are guiltless. they cannot harm us! then master says, yeah i am speaking the truth. the priest says, okay! you are not going to listen to me either.

were a rich family is rulling a country, having the highest standard of living. the boy belonged to this family is fallen in love with a maid servant. he begins to like her and aspired to mary. his family members give the nagative response when he tells it to them. they start to make fun saying, which thing have you liked? do you know that we will make a bound of your marriage in the rich family. that boy feels wrost. he cannot marry a maid servant because of his family. and he marries with another aristocratic girl under families coercion. the maid servant grieved on this. her heart is broken. she is thinking why do the upper class not marry the lower class? are we not human beings? thinking it she commits suicide on a day. because she was not getting courage to forget it. on the other side, that rich family was happy in their family. they were not getting any problem. that maid servant's mother is feeling very bad, seeing it. she wanted to take revenge for her daughters death. she is a witch who knows how to enchant. and she could curse anyone. now she goes out of that aristocratic mension. she begins to speak, i cursh all of you! the new burn daughter in your family will be pig faced. no one will marry her. all people give dissapproval to her. in the same way, she will irritate her life. she will not be healed at that time until someone accepts her. and it is incredible. curshing it, that witch leaves from there with broken heart. now it is seen that time continues to pass. many years were passed. and there is always the birth of a boy five times according to the generations in that wealthy family. it is clear that wealthy family used to select the brides out of their family. now the recent boy's marriage is also held. and all are excepting that they will begot a boy. but the daughter is born in their house. and she is exactly the same as witch had cursed. her ears and nose are like pig. her mother is scared, seeing it. but her husband explains her, we will find remedy soon! they named her penelope. the baby girl is pretty but her face used to look mysterious as such. they also attempt that they may have the plastic surgery of their daughter. so her face may be reshaped. but doctors say it is critical! it means plkastic surgery cannot be proceed. there is life threat of penelope in it.

continue in the next edditon.... ....
....

Amarabhilash